Glimpses into Life Through the Bible

2. 'Satanic Verses' in the Bible

Glimpses into Life Through the Bible

2. 'Satanic Verses' in the Bible

Samuel Amirtham & Israel Selvanayagam

2012

Glimpses into Life Through the Bible: 2. *'Satanic Verses' in the Bible* —Published by Rev. Dr. Ashish Amos of the Indian Society for Promoting Christian Knowledge (ISPCK), Post Box 1585, 1654 Madarsa Road, Kashmere Gate, Delhi-110006.

ISBN: 978-81-8465-200-0

Laser typeset by **ISPCK,** Post Box 1585,
1654 Madarsa Road, Kashmere Gate, Delhi-110006
Tel: 23866322, 23866323
e-mail–ashish@ispck.org.in • ella@ispck.org.in

website-www.ispck.org.

Contents

Preface to the Series

→▶━◆◆◆━◀← →▶━◆◆◆━◀←

*W*e regard this as a privilege to connect with average English speaking Christians. While biblical scholarship is steered to deeper, broader and higher avenues with ever increasing sophistication, Christians in the pews, worshiping Sunday after Sunday, and listening to preacher after preacher, continue to remain in ignorance about the way the Bible has to be approached and its message appropriated. In spite of all our exhortation, pastors seem to have other priorities in ministry than reading the Bible and praying with them. Priests of Jesu-Baal, the growing cult all over the world with different labels, flashing images and manipulative techniques of mass media, appear to be flourishing in terms of five star life-styles and more-star wealth. When challenged, they say that theologians and Bible scholars mislead people with their worldly wisdom and cunning methods. Of course we do not want to continue in the word-game or battle with them. There is clear and frequent warning against false prophets in the Bible. But when trained theologians or pastors and fundamentalist preachers blame one another as false prophets, we have no other option than to leave for God and God's judgment!

This booklet is the second of a series of at least 12 booklets we have decided to produce. We, as a duo have had previous experience of writing similar booklets but in the language of Tamil. Starting from 1980 and completing 20 booklets in 2003, some of them have undergone several reprints and revisions. Since then they have been classified into two volumes and published with the same title, i.e., *Thirumaraikku Thirumpuvom* (Return to the Word of God, Vol. I in 2008 and Vol. II in 2011) by the Arasaradi Publications of the Tamilnadu Theological Seminary, Madurai. There have been a few asking for the English translation of these booklets. However, we are not in a position to do it and therefore we leave it for others to do.

In a slightly different style and approach, more engaging and detailed, we have come forward to produce these booklets. We the writers are different in age, background, aptitude, experience and perspectives. However, we have a unique kind of blood relation, i.e. bound together by the sacramental blood of Jesus Christ. It is our joy and hope that pastors and congregation members, as individuals and groups, engage with us and with God, reading them and feed-backing to us. In a context of fundamentalist literature littered everywhere that has created a confusing and stumbling jumble, please do not ignore ours even if you reject them after reading! Be assured of our prayerful faith journey with you.

When we approached with the proposal, Dr. Ashish Amos, the General Secretary of the ISPCK, responded positively and happily. We are grateful to him and his staff team who have played different roles to get these booklets into your hands. All glory and honour be to our Triune God, the greatest companion in our journey.

Samuel Amirtham & Israel Selvanayagam
Advent 2011

'Satanic Verses' in the Bible

WELCOME

*D**ear Reader,* the title of this booklet might have shocked you. This title is used by no means to devalue the Bible but to enhance right understanding of the variety of manifestations of Satan. It reminds us the controversial novel *Satanic Verses* by the India born British author Salman Rushdie. When the novel appeared in 1988 it stirred the feelings of the Muslims all over the world. There was a decree issued on the life of Rushdie by Ayotalla Koymeni, the then supreme leader of Iran. Though the novel itself was a hard reading for an average reader, the story was built on the traditional view that while Prophet Mohammed was receiving the divine revelation word by word Satan intruded and consequently few verses of Satan got a place in the Holy Qur'an. It was concerning three goddesses of Mecca whose existence and intercession the Prophet affirmed in order to compromise with his Meccan enemies. Consequently, the followers of the Prophet were relieved from persecution. However, later the concerned verses were either denied by the Prophet himself or removed in the later editions of the Qur'an. Scholars still debate about the history of this tradition. However, the timing of the release of this novel coincided with a crucial moment. Anti-Muslim sentiments were spreading world over, particularly in the West. While Islamic mission in the West was getting vigorous and conversion to Islam was on the increase, Muslims were presented in the media as cruel, uncivilized and terrorist. Therefore, understandably the novel provoked Muslims. There were riots and protest marches in which copies of the novel were burned. In India too there were riots and even killings.

The Bible has to be read carefully and interpreted meaningfully. It may be shocking yet revealing and even correcting for a Christian to realize that there are 'Satanic Verses' in the Bible. As we have stressed in the last booklet in this series, we need to be aware of the devil's advices which are misleading. Even at the time of creation, the devil tries to distort the vision of God's purpose for human life. What Job's friends said, though sensible, angered God! During Jesus' temptation in the wilderness the devil was using scriptures for deviating God's purpose for life. We need to understand the nature of Satan's interpretation. Even the dearest disciple Peter was not free from the devil's inspiration that resulted in Jesus rebuking him. There are attractive ways of presenting and interpreting verses from the Bible which may be misleading. Then we have to learn how to approach the Bible and interpret its message for our living today and for understanding our society and the world at large. Therefore, we ask you to read this whole booklet patiently and prayerfully. We do pray for you that you are guided by the Holy Spirit into all truth.

Who is Satan?

You might immediately remember plays in Sunday School functions in which Satan is projected as a horned, black-hooded or painted, male with vampire teeth. Today there are people to object this projection for the following valid reasons:

1. Activists of animal rights want to see the good side of animals. They will argue that in most cases horned animals are more kind towards their partners and kids than many humans. It is true, is not?

2. Blacks would point out the racist prejudice behind this projection. Can there not be whites as Satan? What about other coloured people?

3. Those who are critical of patriarchy and work for women rights may be bit relieved to see that at least in such rare

occasions males are projected in bad light. At the same time, some of them and others may ask for a projection, gender free!

4.   Vampire teeth signify the horrible nature of Satan. Today, some persons or certain countries are artistically projected as having vampire teeth as they implicitly eat up into the rights and resources of the poor and marginalized in the world. Can we deny that?

As such, how do we answer the question, who is Satan? We do not want to give a pre-mature answer by giving a simple image or understanding. Certainly the Bible does not help us to stereotype the image of Satan. Then either we have to give more than one answer or raise different kinds of questions!

What does the word 'Satan' mean? What are his other Names?

The word has Hebrew and Greek roots, respectively, *Sâtân* and *Satanas*. It is used in the sense of someone who opposes or an adversary (Num. 22:22; 1 Sam. 19: 22; 1 Kgs. 11: 14). The associated names are devil, evil spirit and demon. Then there are some peculiar words that suggest the characteristics of Satan.

The Greek translation of the Hebrew Bible (LXX) uses the word demon to describe heathen gods or foreign deities who led people to evil practices and who demanded blood sacrifices (Lev. 17: 7; Deut. 32: 17; 2 Chr. 11: 15; Ps. 96: 5; 106: 37; 65: 3, 11; in some cases they may be translated as 'hairy ones'). Such sacrifice was prohibited for Israelites. The corresponding word is translated as marmots in Is. 13: 21; 34: 14 and we may infer that the image of the demon was that of a strange animal. The name Azazel in Lev. 16: 8, 10 has the meaning of a scapegoat and demon in a desert region. Fowler's snare, deadly pestilence, terrors, arrows, plague, etc mentioned in Psalm 91 may be taken as manifestations of demon.

An evil spirit from God was tormenting king Saul (1 Sam. 16: 14-23) and this suggests that God controls evil spirits and use them at will.

Satan was noted the chief of the army of demons. NT writers believed that demons were Satan's minions. Even Jesus was criticized for having the prince of demons (Mk. 3: 22; Jn. 7:20; 10:20). Unclean spirits were possessing persons and roaming around in waterless places (Mt 12: 43). Pagans sacrifice to demons, and Christians should have nothing to do with them (1 Cor. 10: 20).

'The rest of mankind who survived these plagues still did not renounce the gods their hands had made, or ceased their worship of demons and of idols fashioned from gold, silver, bronze, stone, and wood, which cannot see or hear or walk' (Rev. 9: 20). Evil spirits and ghosts are also associated with the power and function of Satan.

Here when we say 'Satanic Verses' we are concerned not only with the exact words of Satan, devil, demon or evil spirit though that is our main focus, but we will also deal with the strange ways by which he/it operates in human minds and in the society and the world at large.

Who is Satan?

The book of Job chapters 1& 2 have the following detailed description of Satan. Standing as one among the heavenly hosts, he seems to play the role of an advocate before God against God's devotees.

> The day came when the members of the court of heaven took their places in the presence of the Lord, and the Adversary, Satan, was there among them. The Lord asked him where he had been. 'Ranging over the earth', said the Adversary, 'from end to end.' The Lord asked, 'Have you considered my servant Job? You will find no one like him on earth, a man of blameless and upright life, who fears God and set his face against wrongdoing. 'Has not Job good reason to be god fearing?' answered the Adversary. Have you not hedged him round on every side with your protection, him and his family and all his possessions? Whatever he does you bless, and everywhere his herds have increased beyond measure. But just stretch out your hand and touch all that he has, and see if he will not curse you to your face.' 'Very well,' said the Lord. All that he has is in your power; only the man himself you must not touch.' With that the Adversary left the Lord's presence (1: 6-12).

> Once again the day came when...(*same as above*). You incited me to ruin him without cause, but he still holds fast to his integrity.' The Adversary replied, 'Skin for

skin! To save himself there is nothing a man will withhold. 'But just reach out your hand and touch his bones and his flesh, and see if he will not curse you to your face.' The Lord said to the Adversary, 'So be it. He is in your power; only spare his life.' When the Adversary left the Lord's presence he afflicted Job with running sores from the soles of his feet to the crown of his head…, and Job took a piece of a broken pot to scratch himself as he sat among the ashes (2: 1-8).

Interestingly, in the book of Job Satan never appears again. To follow the sequence of the story, Job's wife seems to play the role of Satan when she tells her husband, 'Why do you still hold fast to your integrity? Curse God, and die' (2: 9). Job's answer is very polite, as you know. Immediately follows is the coming of Job's three friends! Do their opinions and arguments also suggest the mind of Satan? We will come back to this in due course.

How did Satan Originate?

*I*s he more powerful than God? Or is God not good enough to protect God's children from the influence of Satan? These questions have been raised for ages and no one has suggested a conclusive answer. With reference to the Bible, to experience and fierce debates, Christian tradition has at least the following explanations:

1. Sons of the fallen angels (Gen. 6). How and why did the angels fall? This was because some angels refused to bow down before the humans created by God, as Islam holds?

2. Lucifer (light bearer), the Latin name for the planet Venus. In Is. 14:12 Babylon is said to be the bright morning star fallen from heaven and lay prostrate on earth. In Babylon morning light was associated with certain stars and their

9

corresponding deities. When the 72 disciples reported back to Jesus that even demons had submitted to them, he said, 'I saw Satan fall, like lightning, from heaven' (Lk. 10: 18). This was to encourage them. In a different scene, 'a star that had fallen from heaven to earth, and the star was given the key to the shaft of the abyss' (Rev. 9: 1). More dramatic is the following:

Then war broke out in heaven; Michael and his angels fought against the dragon. The dragon with his angels fought back, but he was too weak, and they lost their place in heaven. The great dragon was thrown down, that ancient serpent who led the whole world astray, whose name is the Devil, or Satan; he was thrown down to the earth, and his angels with him (Rev.12: 7- 9).

The counter-figure to the fallen morning star angels is Jesus as the star of the dawn (22: 16). What do all these verses suggest? It seems the heavenly angels were prone to pride and sin and they fall from their glory and become the hosts of Satan. But in this world he is represented by oppressive Empires that wage war with the righteous.

3. Personification of evil emotions. Though God is spirit God is personified with eyes, ears, face, hands etc. Likewise, the evil power, opposite to the good power, i.e., God, gets personified and called Satan or Devil

4. An adversary that God created in order to test human steadfastness and faithfulness to God. God is so democratic that he created his own opposite party!

5. Humans are created with freewill. They can err and go astray. They can develop superstitious beliefs and practices such as dividing the time as auspicious and inauspicious. As someone has put it, 'whereas God created the *fact* of freedom, humans perform the *acts* of freedom. God made evil possible; creatures make it actual.'

    Misuse of the freewill over generations of millions of years, have developed into an invisible force that has the capacity to lead humans astray.

6. Unknown agency for misleading humans. They cannot ask the question why this agency was created or allowed in the first place. That is a mystery. They are supposed to live with care and full alert.

7. Evil signifies the opposite side of goodness and truth, and it does not have its own existence. Just like without darkness there cannot be light, without badness and untruth there cannot be goodness and truth. That means, though it has the moral power to make humans fall, it does not have an everlasting life. Evil will eventually be destroyed and now it cannot be done without destroying free will

8. God must have a purpose for creating or allowing the evil to emerge and as finite humans we cannot understand God's infinite knowledge.

Now you can suggest new ideas and solutions if they come to your mind. But neglecting the question about some sort of existence of Satan amounts to allow him to overpower you and to blind your mind so that you accept everything, even some of the dubious verses of the scripture!

How does Satan look like? Where is he Located?

In most cases, Satan's work is narrated without telling anything about his image. For example, in Jesus' temptation story we read 'the devil said to him…led him..took him.' Can you imagine that he did these by appearing as a giant figure?

In the garden Eden, the devil appeared in the form of a serpent 'which was the most cunning of all the creatures the Lord had made' (Gen. 3:1). Then you may ask, how can a serpent speak? As you know, many thinking Christians have suggested that we should not take such stories literally. They are mythical stories telling through pictures and imagery profound truths about human life.

Roaring lion is another image used by Peter (1 Pet. 5:8). The meaning is almost self-explanatory. He is asking the Christians to stand firm in the face of persecution.

The enigmatic title 'Synagogue of Satan' (Rev. 2:9; 3:9) has baffled scholars as much as believers. Read in the context, it signifies a group of Jews who refused the identity 'Jew' for Christians as most of them came from the Jewish fold. On the whole, both Jews and Christians share the same fight against the imperial Rome in the book of Revelation. However, when a zealot group creates tension within the fighting camp then they play the role of Satan. They weaken the position of the faithful, both Jews and Christians.

The title 'Seat and home of Satan' (2:13) also has puzzled readers and different suggestions are made. One is that here the 'seat' or 'throne' denotes an altar dedicated to one of the Greco-Roman gods or goddesses. But more convincing explanation is that it is the seat of the Roman governor. The context is persecution of Christians by the Roman authorities for their refusal to accept the Roman Emperor as Lord and the imperial cult with all its attendant evil practices. One faithful person in Pergamum, Antipas, was martyred and even then the Christian community there stood firm in their faith.

What are the Ways in which Satan Acts?

He moved David to number the people (1 Chro. 21: 1). When God allowed and even asked Moses to count people (particularly in the book of Numbers), why was it not acceptable when David did? Answers differ. One most probable reason was that as king ordained by God, David should have relied on God, not on the numerical strength of the people. Here Satan worked implicitly giving pressure in the mind of David.

He stands at the right hand of Joshua the high priest accusing him while the angel of the Lord standing on the left side. The angel countered him saying that the Lord would silence him (Zech. 3: 1- 2). The situation is precarious when the faithful community rebuilds itself under the fragile leadership of Joshua, the high priest.

The psalmist thinks it is a calamity to have Satan stand at one's right side accusing the righteous (Ps. 109:6). The Lord's judgment will expose his vile.

Asking Jesus' permission to sift and destroy Peter's fragile faith (Lk. 22: 31). Jesus tells him that he never allowed him to do so. Jesus seems to have secret conversation with the devil!

Inducing or entering into Judas to betray Jesus (Lk. 22: 3; Jn. 13: 2, 27). Those who read all the accounts of Judas in the Gospels will realize that the main motive of Judas betraying Jesus was not thirty silver coins. The coins became nothing when he learned that Jesus was convicted to be crucified. Judas, like few other disciples who were probably sympathetic to the Zealots, wanted Jesus to act more dramatically, overthrow the Roman Empire and establish the kingdom of God. They were like Peter who openly declared that Jesus should not suffer! Judas thought that Jesus would escape when he was arrested!

The devil sins from the beginning (1 Jn. 3: 8, 10) 'This is what shows who are God's children and who are the devil's; anyone who fails to do what is right and loves his fellow Christian he is not a child of God.'

The devil could deceive Christians, as anti-Christ who could not affirm incarnation but only reality in the spiritual realm. You might have heard sermons emphasizing more on spiritual matters than on what Jesus of Nazareth did on the ground, identifying with sinners and victims of manifold oppression and embracing the excluded. Therefore one needs to have the spirit of discernment to distinguish between real Christ and anti-Christ (1 Jn. 4: 1, 3, 6).

There are 'principalities and powers' (Eph. 2: 2; 6: 12), potentially able to separate Christians from God (Rom. 8: 38f; 1 Cori. 15: 24; Col. 2: 8-15). They are everywhere including in the atmosphere. There are different opinions among the Christians about this topic. Do they mean real spirits or unjustly ruling authorities? We do not want to prejudice your thinking, therefore you are free to form your own view.

'The prince of this world approaches; he has no right over me', said Jesus (Jn. 14:30). This saying of Jesus has puzzled many Christians. When Jesus is the prince of peace with all power, how can there be yet another prince? Perhaps it has to be taken in a particular sense. Although the universe belongs to God the creator, because of people's choice for wrong options in the world, the world is left to the grip of the devil.

Devil as Beelzebub, the prince of demons, and Jesus is given this title by his Jewish opponents (Mt. 10:25; 12: 24, 27). Jesus refutes their claim saying that their children too exorcise. They will stand against them on the judgment day.

The one who takes away the good seeds sown (Mk. 4:15; Mt. 13: 38f) in Jesus' parable of the sower. Thus we are asked to be vigilant when we preach the word of God because the devil is around to take away the kernel of truth from the hearing or memory of the people.

The devil possessed the mind of Ananias and his wife to hide and lie (Acts 5:3) about the sale of their property.

Satan continues to tempt persons with sexual passions where there is lack of self-control(1 Cori. 7:5).

One Simon was condemned with the words, 'Son of the devil, Greedy, money-minded trying to buy the gift of healing of the Holy Spirit' (Acts 13:10).

Satan hinders the work of the missionaries. Paul says: 'I wanted to visit more than once but Satan thwarted us' (1 Thes. 2:18). In what way did this happen is not explained.

In Paul's time there was a conflict between false apostles and true apostles just like between false prophets and true prophets. Paul has some harsh words to use about the false ones:

> Such people are sham apostles, confidence tricksters masquerading as apostles of Christ. And no wonder! Satan himself masquerades as an angel of light, so it is easy enough for his agents to masquerade as agents of good. But their fate will match their deeds (2 Cori. 11: 13-15)

Today there are accusations and counter-accusations between different types of Christian preachers, pastors and workers. Can you prove the right in an argument or debate? In most times it is more sensible to leave the matter for God to deal with.

While talking about his weakness which was not open to others to see, Paul says,

> To keep me from being unduly elated by the magnificence of such revelations, I was given a thorn

in my flesh, a messenger of Satan sent to buffet me; this was to save me from being unduly elated. Three times I begged the Lord to rid me of it, but his answer was: 'My grace is all you need; power is most fully seen in weakness.' I am therefore happy to boast of my weaknesses, because then the power of Christ will rest upon me. So I am content with a life of weakness, insult, hardship, persecution and distress, all for Christ's sake; for when I am weak, then I am strong (2 Cori. 12: 7-10).

What do you think is the exact 'thorn in the flesh'? Have you heard explanations? There is no conclusive answer! It is widely held that it was a physical or psychic ailment which was believed to be caused by demons. One explanation is that Paul had some opponents within the Christian community and if so they were just like the inhabitants of the occupied land who could become for Israelites 'like a barbed hook in your eye and a thorn in your side' as we read in Numbers 33: 55). Some view it as a nagging thought of immoral nature. How can a saint have such a thought or feeling? Perhaps to avoid further reasoning in this rather sensitive matter, there is a shift to mean it as suffering in mission. Was it an interpolation by someone who wanted to present Paul in saintly light? In any case, even if it was an ailment or nagging thought, for Paul it provided a profound realization of living in constant reliance on God's all sufficient grace.

Paul has some pastoral advice to church leaders and servants of God in general. For instance, he says, a bishop 'must moreover have a good reputation with the outside world, so that he may not be exposed to scandal and be caught in the Devil's snare' (1 Tim. 3:7). And a servant of God, even in the midst of troubles and opposition from those who instigate quarrels,

> must be kindly towards all. He should be a good teacher, tolerant and gentle when he must discipline them who oppose him. God may then grant them a change of heart and lead them to recognize the truth; thus they may come to their senses and escape from the devil's snare in which they have been trapped and held at his will (2 Tim. 2:26).

There is a wonderful advice for creative pastoral behaviour. A pastor, while her/himself not being trapped by the snares of the devil, helps those unruly folk so that they may come out of the snares of the devil. Adding snare to snare strengthens the snare that boosts the devil!

Now you must feel that Satan is active in far more varied ways than you have thought so far. Thinking of only one way as devil's is in fact becoming prone to his cunning snares which he spreads in different contexts in different styles. He can be much more subtle than you would ever imagine. The following instances might shake you to the core!

Sensible but Confused Speech

I*t* is observed by many in different contexts that the so called demons speak the truth and expose crimes and oppression. What is known as shamanism in certain cultures such as in Korea on particular festivals the shaman possessed by a spirit lambasts the rich and those who oppress in the locality. In other cases the so called evil spirits possess particular persons, mostly women, and expose a theft or murder that has taken place and discreetly dealt with following all malpractices. There are cults the origin of which were connected with murders. The spirit of the murdered possessed certain persons and threatened revenge in the form of inflicting pain and loss. The only compromise could be a blood sacrifice to be offered to that spirit every year. Besides, we are told stories of dalit victims in the context of bonded labour who behave in a dramatic way. If the landlord raped one's wife or daughters which sometimes happens, he will get drunk and challenge face to face the landlord throwing on him all filthy words and curses. Or he would chop the banana trees in his garden to express his anger. Then that is not the end of the story. The anti-climax is that he would go to the landlord early in the morning and say sorry for what happened in the previous night when he was drunk. Have you come across similar stories? What is your opinion about such expressions? In any case, such stories help us to understand the behaviour of some demon-possessed in the Bible which is sensible but confused!

If Satan or devil does outright evils it is easy to identify and move away from it. But if it does some good things though unbalanced, then you are in a fix to decide. For example, can you believe that the devil too has faith and trembles out of fear before God? Apostle James says so (Js. 2: 19). His point is faith without action is nothing. Then how many people you think in your knowledge have faith and fear of God in the devil's way?

In the Gospels, in some stories of exorcism paralysing physical conditions are associated with demon possession, like dumbness (Mtt 9:32f; Lk 11:14), blindness and dumbness (Mtt 12:22), epileptic fits (17:14f), deafness and dumbness (Mk 9:17-27; Lk 9:37-43). In one case the condition was one of terrible inner torment (Mtt 15:22; Mk 7:26f). Jesus never tried to analyse the cases as a psychologist or psychoanalyst would do. He accepted the customary beliefs of his day. But he cured all of them thereby demonstrating his power over demons and evil spirits. Do you think there are many Christian exorcists who can do this way without any publicity or advertisement? For Jesus, encountering spirit-possessed persons was incidental and the cure was total.

But there is one interesting category of cases in which we can detect a distinctive condition that seems to reveal a particular social background which had led to strange psycho-somatic symptoms. Perhaps you have not noticed their peculiarity but clubbed them with others. For instance, a man in the Capernaum Synagogue (surely an unusual admission to the divine worship in the first place!), possessed by 'an unclean spirit', encountered Jesus with a collective pronoun and theological affirmation:

> What do you want with *us*, Jesus of Nazareth? Have you come to destroy *us*? I know who you are – the Holy One of God' Mk 1:24). And whenever the people who had evil spirits in them saw him, they would fall down before him and scream, 'You are the Son of God!' (Mk. 3:11).

Such confession was strikingly significant for acknowledging and understanding who Jesus was (cf. Mtt. 3:17; 4:3, 6; 26:63; 27:40, 43). The encounter is even more dramatic in the story of the 'Gerasene Demoniac' (Matt 8:28-34; Mk 5:1-20; Lk 8:26-39) which we will describe in some detail.

The textual variation between the first three Gospels' versions of the story of the 'Gerasene demoniac' (Mtt 8: 28-34; Mk 5:1-20; Lk 8: 26-39) suggest a reworking of different versions of the oral tradition or even of different events or tales.

Matthew's note of 'two men' and their address of Jesus as simply 'Son of God', and Luke's mention of Jesus being met by 'a man from the town' are most significant examples of the variation. For our purpose we take Mark's version which is the longest narrative story in the whole gospel apart from the passion narrative.

Looking through the lens of the above mentioned living stories, one realises how limiting is the neat prose form of such a story in the gospel or at least its translation. As far as our chosen story is concerned, the present prose form is not able to convey the likely idiomatic charm of the encounter of Jesus and the demoniac. When such stories are told in the indigenous languages and local colloquia, there is invariably far more raw poetic power, more pithy expression of the rustic language, often the irony and even sarcasm, the more enigmatic allusiveness in such encounters.

Whether a reconstruction of the story in English is able to convey the original cultural dynamics and linguistic nuances is no doubt questionable. With an acknowledgment of such limitation we suggest the following version (based on the Good News Bible).

On his entry into the territory of Gerasa, Jesus was met by a man who came out of the burial caves there. He had a kind of evil spirit which could not be contained. He would break any chain that people put around his feet. He was so strong that no-one could control him. He was forced to wander around the tombs and hills, yet went on shouting something and expressing his helplessness and resentment by self-torture.

He fell on his knees before Jesus and shouted, 'Hey, Jesus, Son of the Most High God! What do you want with me? For God's sake, please don't you also try to punish me (as the people around do).' Jesus was saying, 'why this pretence, you evil spirit, come out openly'. 'What is your name?' Jesus asked. 'Ha-ha-ha. My name is "Mob" – we are too many' he replied.

He further asked Jesus not to send them away from the region, but to the pigs. When this was granted they entered the herd of two thousand pigs which rushed down the side of the cliff into the lake and were drowned. The herdsmen spread the news. He was sitting there, clothed and in his *right mind*. But people were afraid and asked Jesus to leave their territory. The man whose *right mind* was restored asked Jesus permission to go with him. But Jesus refused and told him to go back to his family and tell them what the Lord had done to him. He did so to the amazement of his hearers.

While there may be no concrete evidence, it is not unreasonable to think that there were many like him in that area and some of them were behind the scene in which the pigs went to their doom. This could be a cathartic expression of a whole community's bottled up resentment or awareness-creating strategy or both. We can even speculate that the owner of the pigs was a prime exploiter. However, in the story only one man is projected openly as a representative of a victim community pushed out to a life of alienation and self-torture. Presumably gaining the label 'mad' involved a long process. The term 'God of the Most High' echoes a Gentile environment (cf. Gen 14:18; Nu 24:16; Acts 16:17), and so pushing Jesus to broaden his boundary (see Mtt 15:21-28) in his ministry of revitalising the liberating movement of Yahweh.

On the whole this does not provide a very neat reconstruction of the story. The story itself suffers from lack of sequence. For instance, Jesus' telling the spirits to come out seems, in this sense, to be not an instant verbal command but a slow communication with encouraging gestures. Jesus recognised the ability of his voluntary client to speak out truth and he encouraged him to come out openly with no more confusion. We will soon refer to few other stories of similar nature in the New Testament..

What lies behind these demons behaving so sensibly, even speaking out the truth perhaps hidden to others? What was the condition of the persons concerned who, despite the confusion inherent in their situation, who seem to disclose an aspiration to speak out not only sensibly, but effectively? Should these stories be taken merely as examples of the fraudulent trickery of the evil one? On the other hand, do western explanations – often based on modern psychological assumptions – really convince? It is important to note that these stories are originally Asian stories and similar stories in present day Asia can help to uncover their particular background and meaning.

Such cases are in the Acts of Apostles also. For instance, the slave girl in Philippi who had 'an evil spirit', followed Paul and his companions shouting, 'these men are servants of the most High God! They announce to you how you can be saved!' (16:18). Further, when the seven sons of Sceva, Jewish High Priest, used the name of Jesus for casting out evil spirits with a vested interest, they in the singular respond: 'Jesus I recognise, Paul I know, but who are you?'(19:15). They/it overpowered the men and the exorcists were running off naked! How sensible evil spirits are they?

Have you witnessed to such events in your life? In fact, it will be good if some spirit-possessed people behave in this way exposing the professional and selfish motives of the exorcists!

What are the Primary Points of Satanic Verses in the Bible?

→❖◈❖◈❖◈❖◈← →❖◈❖◈❖◈◈←

***W**hat* we have looked at so far are about the strange ways of Satan's behaviour and talks. The 'Satanic Verses' in these cases are rather indirect. Now we turn to the more direct verses of the devil although they need some explanation within the context of their occurrence.

Transgress the Limits (Serpent in Eden)

In the story of beginnings, the first human Adam was made and placed in a garden that God planted. Subsequently, 'The Lord God made trees to grow up from the ground, every kind of tree pleasing to the eye and good for food; and in the middle of the garden he set the tree of life and the tree of the knowledge of good and evil' (Gen. 2: 9). God told Adam, 'You may eat from any tree in the garden except from the tree of the knowledge of good and evil; the day you eat from that, you are surely doomed to die (2: 16).' Then Eve was created and given to Adam to be his wife. The above warning probably was communicated to her by Adam. Satan in the form of a serpent asked the woman,

> 'is it true that God has forbidden you to eat from any tree in the garden?' She replied with greater force of the warning: 'we may eat the fruit of any tree in the garden, except for the tree in the middle of the garden. God has forbidden us to eat the fruit of that tree or even to touch it; if we do we shall die.' 'Of course you will not die', said the serpent; 'for God knows that, as soon you eat it, your eyes will be opened and you will be like God himself, knowing both good and evil.' The woman looked at the tree; the fruit would be good to eat; it was pleasing to the eye and desirable for the knowledge it could give. So she took some and ate it; she also gave some to her husband, and he ate it. The eyes of both of them were opened, and they knew that they were naked; so they stitched fig leaves together and made themselves loincloths (3: 2-7).

The story continues with a dialogue between God, Adam, Eve and the serpent and each got punishment. The garden of Eden was closed and sealed.

In the whole of episode, many questions arise and an explanation is needed. We will observe the most important of them:

1. While the tree of life continues until the last part of the last book of the Bible, the tree of the knowledge of good

and evil never comes again. What does it suggest? It makes sense if one says that it is invisibly planted in every life, every context and every relationship.

2. The forbidden fruit has been regarded as sex in some circles. But there is no evidence for that and in fact the Bible is positive about sex and expresses it openly.

3. Eve found the fruit to be good (tasty) to eat, pleasing to the eye and desirable for knowledge. Different kinds of pleasure –physical, sensual and intellectual – are mentioned here, therefore the jealous God withholds these from humans. This explanation too is not acceptable because the Bible is positive about these. That is the reason, though there is a place for renunciation for a select few, the Judeo-Christian tradition is open to physical enjoyment, sensual pleasure and intellectual pursuit.

4. Basically, Adam and Eve did not trust God and disobeyed God's command. Perhaps what the devil said appeared to be more convincing and practical. Why should we blindly obey an authority, be it parents, teachers or God? New Testament writers like Paul have taken the act of disobedience as fundamental and the cause for the sin of the whole human race. They hardly have any sympathy to the difficult position in which Adam and Eve were placed. Certainly they did not deliberately rebel. Adam had faithfully transmitted God's warning and Eve understood fully the implications of neglecting it.

5. Though the question of trust and obedience is important to reckon with, some thinking Christians have suggested

that Adam and Eve transgressed the limit set by God. There was meaning and purpose within the limited life. There was freedom to eat fruit from all the trees in the garden and the water sources were plenty to enjoy drinking and bathing. However, humans were asked to respect the limit set by God, limit of knowing and enjoying. Knowing good and evil is a technical term which means knowing all. The Hebrew words used here for good and evil are used in another context in the book of Genesis. When Abraham's senior servant proposed the marriage of Isaac and Rebecca, her father Bethuel and brother Laban instantly replied, 'Since this is from the Lord, we can say nothing good or evil' (Gen. 24:50).

Living within the limits set by God in all areas of life makes it both challenging and enjoyable. Why only this much stomach, this much energy and this much time to live? One can go on asking such questions. But God has a good purpose for the system and that should be respected. According to the Eden story, when Adam and Eve transgressed the limit aspiring to become all knowing and all powerful, they realized only their nakedness and that resulted in shame and fear. The sense of shame and fear moved God to act in a gracious way.

This message has profound insights into understanding the ills of human life and of societies and nations today. When one crosses the limit of eating in moderation he becomes obese and seeks treatment. He has spoiled the balance between the requirement and available resources and driven some other persons to reel under poverty and malnutrition. This is true of the nations and superpowers as well. One nation's greed and thirst for domination makes other nations weak and vulnerable. In the name of development and modernization natural resources are depleted causing climate changes. Be sure, there is no unlimited resource on the earth. Oil is not unlimited! Satan always tempts with temporal attractions and short term gains which in the long run lead us to destruction. You can apply this to any area in life, from husband-wife relations to the behaviour of government authorities.

Why Job's Friends Were Wrong?

As we have already noted, in the first part of the story of Job, Satan appears to be among the angels in heaven. He travels on the earth and then tries to challenge devout persons' steadfastness. He challenges God too for protecting such upright persons like Job. God accepted the challenge and allowed the devil to inflict pain and suffering for Job. His wife does exactly what Satan expected Job to do: 'Curse God and die'. Job answered, 'You talk as any impious woman might talk. If we accept good from God, shall we not accept evil?' Throughout all this, Job did not utter one sinful word (Job 2: 10). Immediately coming are the three friends of Job. What was their position?

Eliphaz, after praising Job's good life and what he has done to other suffering people jumps into the traditional view: 'those who plough mischief and sow trouble reap no other harvest. They perish at the blast of God; they are shrivelled by the breath of his nostrils' (4: 8-9). He goes on saying many things without any coherence. After Job's reply, Bildad speaks of a better future if Job and his children are really righteous, and this also does not satisfy Job. Then speaks Zophar about the unfathomable nature of the mystery of God and it will be fully and justly revealed in future. None of these friends' talks are unintelligible for Job but they do not suggest a solution to his problems.

In the second round of speeches, Eliphaz asks for some respect for the old age of him and his companions from Job who is relatively younger. He reiterates that the reward for the godless and the wicked will certainly come in future. Bildad and Zophar almost repeat the same point in different words. In the third round, Eliphaz and Bildad indirectly hint that Job is wicked in some way and God's justice is accurate. A transition note says, 'These three men gave up answering Job, for he continued to think himself righteous' (32: 1). Then another friend Elihu starts expressing his feeling of anger at Job because Job appeared to claim more righteous than God. He is equally angry with the three friends older than himself for they did not convince Job to change this perception. Then in his long speech he points out that God is never unjust and Job cannot go on insisting that he is innocent. This he should acknowledge and approach God in penitence. Neither good nor bad affects God and therefore Job must patiently wait upon God to speak. For God is great, greater than anyone's imagination, and his power is revealed in the way the natural world functions. God is absolutely just. 'Therefore mortals pay him reverence, and all who are wise fear him' (37: 24).

Job in some sense acknowledges this though he is not fully content until God directly challenges him and shuts his mouth up!

In the final scene, Elihu is absent, and God tells Eliphaz that he is angry with him and his two friends because they have not spoken as well as Job his servant. And to remedy this they have to offer a whole-offering and then Job will intercede for them. Actually, what wrong have they done? Their arguments are plausible and some of their words overlap with Job's. Whatever may be the author's taste, irony and twist, by blaming Job they have added to his suffering. Do you agree with this? Whatever may be your answer, mind, the friends of Job spoke in continuation of Satan's and Job's wife's speech! Theirs too are 'satanic verses'. They spoilt themselves with their own words instead of behaving better by sitting silent in solidarity with Job. There is a lesson here for all of us. We should never claim that our arguments approximate God's mind and God's plan.

The fact that the arguments and interpretations of Job's friends appeared to be plausible is important to take to heart. This calls for extreme vigilance when people come with simple and reasonable solutions for problems and suffering of others. Centuries later than the production of the book of Job, apostle Paul wrote:

> The Spirit explicitly warns us that in time to come some will forsake the faith and surrender their minds to subversive spirits and demon-inspired doctrines, through the plausible falsehoods of those whose

consciences have been permanently branded (1 Tim. 4: 1-2).

You would recall strange doctrines or explanations of scriptural images put forward by popular preachers. Some would claim that they spoke out of heavenly wisdom as opposed to the worldly wisdom of theologians and trained pastors. After reading the above, what do you think a sensible Christian can do? How to distinguish between satanic verses and divine speech?

Literalist, selfish and quick-fix interpretation which Jesus rejected and countered with alternative Verses

Jesus rejects the literalist and prejudiced approach to the scripture as represented by the devil at the time of his temptation in the wildness. It may appear to be too strong to say that a literalist approach to the scripture is satanic. But the story of Jesus' temptation by the devil makes the point clear. Even scripture is a tool in the hand of Satan to tempt religious people!

> Then the devil took him to the holy city, and set him on the parapet of the temple. 'If you are the Son of God', he said, 'throw yourself down; for scripture says, "He will give his angels in charge of you, and they will support you in their arms, for fear you should strike your foot against a stone".' Jesus answered him, 'Scripture also says, "You are not to put the Lord your God to the test"' (Mtt. 4:5-7; also see Lk. 4:9-12).

The devil is quoting Ps. 91:11,12. Jesus is countering this way of seeking a literalist meaning by quoting Deut. 6:16. In the other two temptations also, Jesus counters the argument by quoting Deut. 8:3 ('not by bread alone') and Deut. 6:13 ('Serve your Lord God alone'). What the devil had quoted in these temptations is not mentioned. It is reasonable, however, to infer that the devil might have pointed out the food miraculously brought by God for the Israelites in the wilderness when he asked Jesus to command stones to become bread. Likewise he might have pointed out verses, which promise power and authority for those who sought God's help when he asked Jesus to bow down before him. In any case Jesus' counter-quotations are very appropriate.

You might have heard many times that preachers quote the scripture and tell God that things should happen accordingly. You have promised this, so be it so to me. You have done this to your people in the Bible, therefore let it be done to my life or the life of the people in this home. You might want to be polite, not to offend a servant of God. If Jesus did it what would have happened? And with reference to similar success stories or miraculous events, the by-passers at the cross asked Jesus to come down and save himself. If he could not save himself how could he save others? Such reasoning is going on all the time. Don't you think we have to muster some courage to challenge the devil by pointing out alternatives?

Those of Conservative Piety with Fanatic Mode as Children of the Devil

Jesus had all the time controversy with those conservative Jewish leaders who refused to be open to see what God was doing new in Jesus Christ. When they were not able to understand what Jesus was saying and doing, not able to love him, they became very murderous. At this point Jesus told them,

> Your father is the devil and you choose to carry out your father's desires. He was a murderer from the beginning, and is not rooted in the truth; there is no truth in him. When he tells a lie he is speaking his own language, for he is a liar and father of lies (Jn. 8: 44).

Just like he rejected the above way of the devil's approach to the scripture, Jesus also rejected the way the Pharisees and Scribes interpreted the laws very minutely with complex ramifications. Jesus says,

> Alas for you, scribes and Pharisees, hypocrites! You pay tithes of mint and dill and cumin; but you have overlooked the weightier demands of the law - justice, mercy, and good faith. It is these you should have practised, without neglecting the others. Blind guides! You strain off a midge, yet gulp down a camel! (Mtt. 23:23, 24).

The spirit of the Pharisees and Scribes seems to haunt the minds of many Christians today when they debate for hours on the right form of baptism etc. without taking the weightier matters of justice and liberation seriously. Or they might insist on giving tithe to them without mentioning justice in the society. Or they may discuss the implications of the last judgment for Hindus and Muslims without taking seriously the imperative to love them.

Elsewhere Jesus points out how the readers of the scriptures can miss the central point of their witness.

> You study the scriptures diligently, supposing that in having them you have eternal life; their testimony points to me, yet you refuse to come to me to receive that life (Jn. 5:39, 40).

Even after years of reading and searching the Bible one may not come to have a grip of this fundamental witness. Therefore, reading the Bible without a proper perspective is rejected by Jesus as much as he rejected the literalist approach.

You should not suffer, Jesus! - Peter

It was following the right confession of who Jesus was, and an attestation by Jesus that it was revealed to Peter by the heavenly Father. Then Jesus began to make clear to his disciples that he had to go to Jerusalem, and endure great suffering at the hands of some Jewish authorities, to be put to death and to be raised again. Subsequently, this dialogue happened between Jesus and Peter

> At this Peter took hold of him and began to rebuke him: 'Heaven forbid!' he said. 'No, Lord this shall never happen to you.' Then Jesus turned and said to Peter, 'Out of my sight, Satan; you are a stumbling block to me. You think as men think, not as God thinks (Mt. 16: 22, 23).

Have you ever noticed a sudden turn of Peter, being an instrument of the heavenly Father to speak the truth, then drifting to be the instrument of the devil? Normally, when we find someone saying or doing right things at particular moments, we think they are always right. This could be exploited by them and can prove to be dangerous. You might have heard stories of sectarian leaders misleading people even to death by marking certain day for the second coming of Jesus. You should have heard ample number of times from fundamentalist preachers that success, prosperity and promotion alone are blessings of God. If one is truly committed to be a disciple of Christ in today's world, it is hard to avoid suffering. If one is tempted to give up the path taken and to prefer an easier way then one should be aware of the devil!

How to Deal with Satanic Verses?

⇢⊱⬥⊰⇠ ⇢⊱⬥⊰⇠

*N*ow we have fairly a comprehensive picture of Satan or Devil, the head or sum total of all demons, unseen powers of affliction and evil spirits. We have seen the variety of ways Satan functions and the variety of ways he speaks. We are not fully certain about the origin and purpose of Satan either created or allowed to develop in the world by a good and almighty God. However, we have no right to be skeptical and cynical about it. We live in a mysterious world and yet we are not supposed to abdicate our responsibilities. Needed fundamentally is an acute awareness of God's presence and mindfulness of Satan's snares.

While we are not clear about the origin of Satan and about his relationship with God, we have the assurance in the Bible that finally Satan will be defeated. In the meantime, the faithful engages in a constant fight with him. Jesus came to overthrow the works of the devil (1 Jn. 3:8; Heb.2:14). His disciples won partial victory over the demons. He said, 'Now is the hour of judgment for this world; now shall the prince of this world be driven out' (Jn. 12: 31; also read 16: 11). He also said that those who are not able to identify Jesus in the hungry, naked, stranger etc share a curse that they will go from his sight to 'the eternal fire that is ready for the devil and his angels' (Mtt. 25: 41). Paul's mission among the Gentiles was 'to open their eyes and to turn them from darkness to light, from the dominion of Satan to God so that they may obtain forgiveness of sins' (Acts. 26: 18). 'Since the children share in flesh and blood, he (Jesus) too shared in them, so that by dying he might break the power of him who had death at his command, that is, the devil' (Heb. 2: 14). And the son of God appeared for the very purpose of undoing the devil's work of sinning (1 Jn. 3: 8). Paul concludes a long letter with the words 'the God of peace will soon crush Satan beneath your feet' (Rom. 16: 20). All these verses unanimously suggest that in different ways there is a process of weakening the power of Satan and then of destroying him.

John in his vision of the future saw the dragon, the ancient serpent, devil or Satan was locked in an abyss for a thousand years (Rev. 20: 1-3) and then, after a period of his seduction and war, finally,

> Their seducer, the Devil, was flung into the lake of fire and sulphur, where the beast and the false prophet had been flung to be tormented day and night for ever (20: 10).

In the meantime, the faithful are called to live with care and full alert. If the devil appears only in the form of a black-hooded, double-horned male with a vampire teeth or a terrifying ghost of shadow we can easily identify. But he and his agents can transform themselves into angels of light (2 Cori. 11: 14). They can appear to be our friends just like Job's and their words can be sensible and arguments plausible.

Those who feel they have to live in constant fight with the devil and all his principalities can find the following advice of the apostle as useful and encouraging:

> Finally, find your strength in the Lord, in his mighty power. Put on the full armour provided by God, so that you may be able to stand firm against the stratagems of the devil. For our struggle is not against our human foes, but against cosmic powers, against the authorities and potentates of this dark age, against the superhuman forces of evil in the heavenly realms. Therefore, take up the armour of God; then you will be able to withstand them on the evil day and, after doing your utmost, to stand your ground. Stand fast, I say. Fasten on the belt of truth; for a breastplate put on integrity; let the shoes on your feet be the gospel of peace, to give you firm footing; and, with all these, take up the great shield of faith, with which you will be able to quench all the burning arrows of the evil one. Accept salvation as your helmet, and sword which the Spirit gives you, the word of God. Constantly ask God's help in prayer, and pray always in the power of the Spirit. To this end keep watch and persevere, always interceding for all God's people (Ephe. 6: 10-18).

The long list provides food for thought for many days. To add, Paul notes that when God allows us to be tested it will not be beyond our power and there will be some provision to escape (1 Cori. 10: 13). James says that God opposes the arrogant and gives grace to the humble. 'Submit then to God. Stand up to the devil, and he will turn and run' (Js. 4:7). In the context of persecution Peter advises: 'Stand up to him (devil), firm in your faith, and remember that your fellow Christians in this world are going through the same kinds of suffering' (1 Pet. 5: 9). You may like to take each of the above and meditate in the light of the 'satanic verses and actions' in the Bible.

Since Satan is nearby watching every moment of our life, we are advised not to give any foothold for him. 'If you are angry, do not be led into sin; do not let sunset find you nursing your anger; and give no foothold to the devil' (Ephe. 4:26f). 'For Satan must not be allowed to get the better of us; we know his viles all too well' (2 Cori. 2: 11).

Where we find people talking some sense but not sharing the spirit of the sufferer we should remember the friends of Job and God's anger against them. When we encounter people who speak the truth but in a confused way, we should help them to come out and be open and clear.

Finally, the most difficult moment to deal with is when Satan handles the scripture and interprets its verses. We have pointed out how Jesus responded. Jesus exposed the selfish and temporal motive of the devil and quoted other verses to point out the alternative. This is the way we are called to follow.

www.ingramcontent.com/pod-product-compliance
Lightning Source LLC
Chambersburg PA
CBHW050835180626
46814CB00004B/1632